A MESSAGE TO PARENTS

It is of vital importance for parents to read good books to young children in order to aid the child's psychological and intellectual development. At the same time as stimulating the child's imagination and awareness of his environment, it creates a positive relationship between parent and child. The child will gradually increase his basic vocabulary and will soon be able to read books alone.

Brown Watson has published this series of books with these aims in mind. By collecting this inexpensive library, parent and child are provided with hours of pleasurable and profitable reading.

Teddy
and Baby Bear

by Maureen Spurgeon
Illustrated by Pamela Storey

Brown Watson

ENGLAND

It was the day of the Teddy Bears' Picnic! Everyone in Bear Village had been busy. The picnic food was ready and the playing fields were marked out ready for games later on.

Teddy was enjoying himself already! He was helping Barry Bear to put paper cups and plates on a long, wooden table. Soon everyone would be ready for the picnic feast. What fun they would have!

"You're such a help, Teddy," smiled Teacher Bear, as she carried bottles of milk and fruit squash to the table. "Could you do a very special job for me? It really would be a great help."

"What sort of job?" asked Teddy.
"Well," said Teacher Bear, "my sister
is coming to help at the picnic, and
we need someone sensible to look
after her little bear, Baby Boo."

"There they are," cried Teacher Bear,
before Teddy could answer.
"Hello, Bonny. Hello, Baby Boo."
Teddy Bear blinked. He had never
seen any bear who looked quite as
sweet as Baby Boo!

"Now, Baby Boo," Teacher went on, "you play with Teddy while Mummy helps with the picnic. You don't mind, do you?" Baby Boo put a paw to her mouth and shook her head. She did not mind at all!

"What a good bear you are," smiled her mummy, patting Baby's furry head. "Just see she doesn't get dirty," she told Teddy.

"That's right!" nodded Teacher. "See she doesn't get dirty."

Baby Boo smiled up at Teddy and took hold of his paw. He didn't know quite what to do. All his friends seemed to be much too busy to stop and talk, and he couldn't see Mummy or Daddy Bear.

"Hey, Teddy!" came the voice of Baker Bear. "Like to come and help blow up a few balloons?"

"Hear that, Baby Boo?" grinned Teddy. "You won't get dirty watching me blowing up balloons."

But Baby Boo did not seem very interested in balloons. What she wanted was to see what was inside a big flower pot!
"No, Baby Boo!" cried Teddy Bear. "Don't get yourself dirty!"

Poor Teddy! He didn't see the tin of whitewash Painter Bear had brought to mark out a game of hopscotch on the grass. How Baby Boo laughed to see Teddy covered with big, white blobs!

"Here's a cloth," cried Baker Bear.
"Let's try and get you clean, Teddy."
But Teddy could not stop! Baby Boo
was already toddling off towards a big
basket of fat, juicy strawberries . . .
"Don't get dirty!" cried Teddy.

SPLOSH! Teddy shut his eyes tight. Then he opened them again. He let out a deep breath. Baby Boo was not at all dirty. HE was covered in bright red splodges of strawberries!

Baby Boo laughed so much that Billy
and Bella Bear came over to see
what the joke was. Then they saw
Teddy. "What happened?" grinned
Billy. He and Bella thought Teddy
looked so funny!

"It's Baby Boo!" growled Teddy. "I'm supposed to see that she doesn't get dirty! Teacher is counting on me!"
"Well, take her across to the swings," Bella suggested. "She won't get dirty there."

That sounded a good idea to Teddy.
Then Baby Boo decided she wanted
a drink at the water fountain.
"Mind that puddle!" warned Teddy
Bear. "Don't get yourself dirty!"

SPLASH! Baby Boo didn't step into the puddle, but Teddy Bear did! Baby Boo looked down at her clean paws and her clean clothes. Then she looked at Teddy, and started laughing again.

Baby Boo didn't stop to see how angry Teddy was. She had seen a big tub of sawdust that Mummy Bear had brought for the lucky dip. It was just inside a big tent, and Baby Boo headed straight for it.

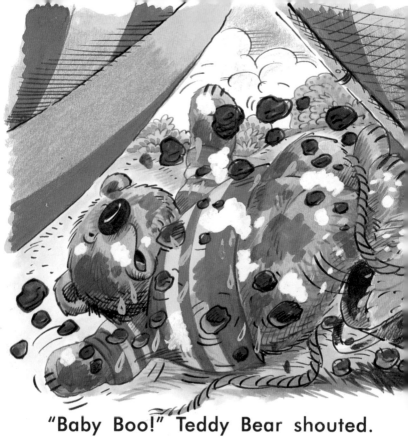

"Baby Boo!" Teddy Bear shouted. "Come here!" He dashed into the tent after her. The next thing he knew, there was a shower of sawdust, grass and earth flying about. The tent fell down around him.

He could hear voices outside.
"What's happened to the tent?"
"Didn't Teddy Bear go inside?"
"Teddy? But I asked him to look after
Baby Boo! He was supposed to see
she didn't get dirty!" said Teacher.

"Baby Boo?" said Baker Bear. "She walked straight past the tent."
There was silence. Slowly, very slowly, and with bears pulling and pushing and prodding him, Teddy Bear crawled out.

Nobody knew what to say.
"Teddy!" gasped Mummy Bear at last.
"What HAVE you been doing?"
"I've been looking after Baby Boo,"
Teddy protested, "making sure she
didn't get dirty!"

"My little Baby Boo?" said her
mummy. "Look at her! She's kept
herself BEAUTIFULLY clean!"
"Yes, but . . ." began poor Teddy.
"YOU'RE covered with sawdust and
muddy splashes!" said Teacher.

"And there's sticky strawberries on your fur!" said Baby Boo's mummy. "To say nothing of all that white-wash!" sighed Mummy Bear. "Oh, Teddy! On the day of the Teddy Bears' Picnic, too!"

"Wait a minute," said Baker Bear.
"Teddy DID look after Baby."
"And he made sure she didn't get dirty," added Barry Bear.
"And there's no harm done," said Daddy Bear.